The Pancake King

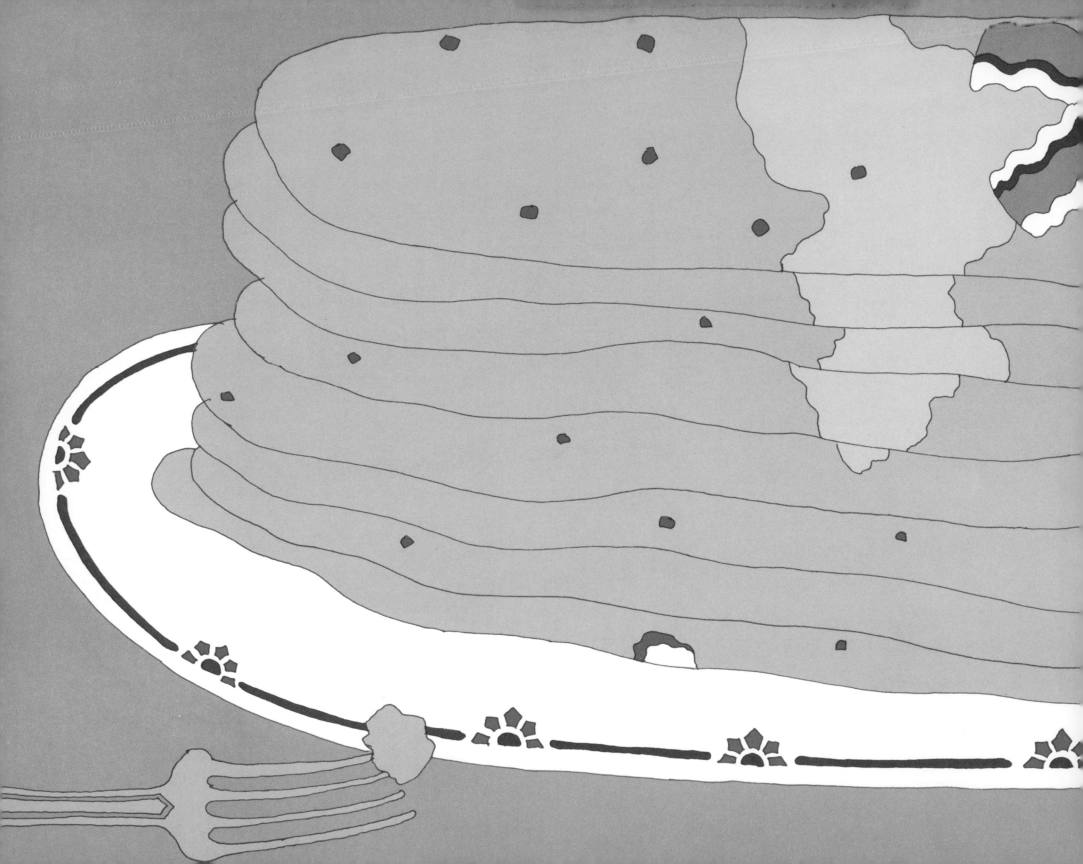

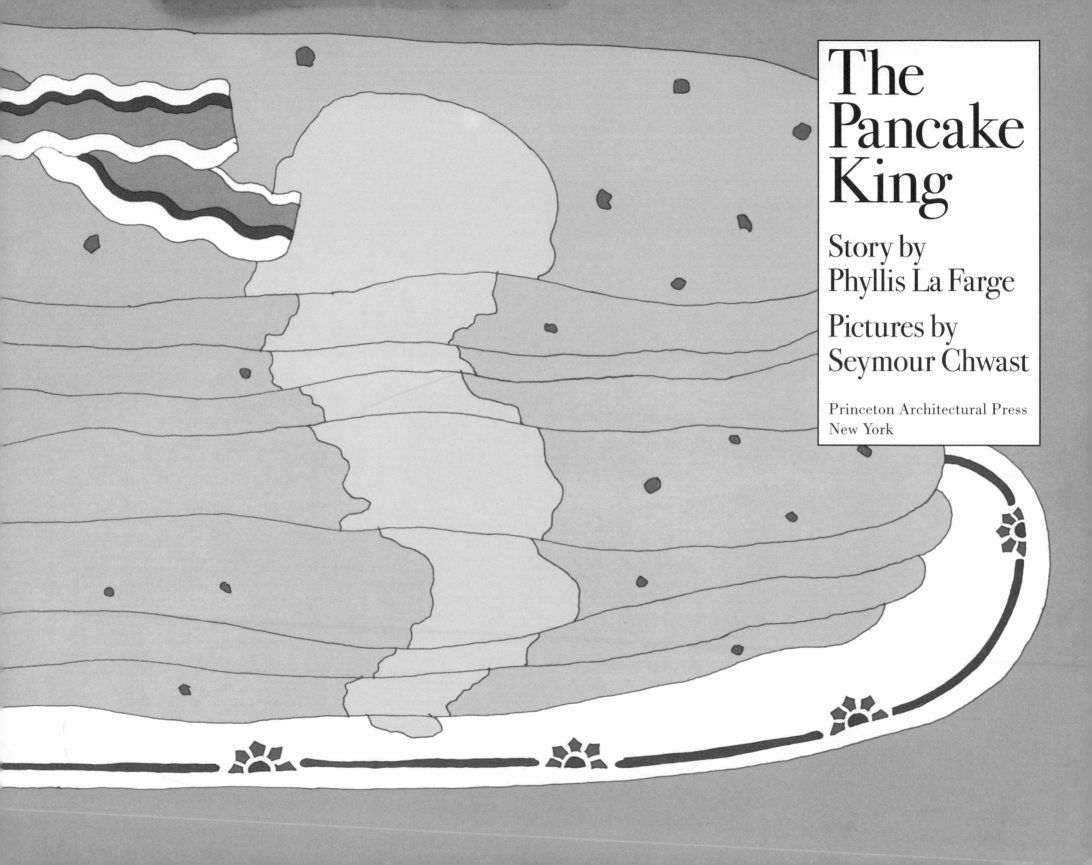

The Pancake King

Story by
Phyllis La Farge

Pictures by
Seymour Chwast

Princeton Architectural Press
New York

Published by
Princeton Architectural Press
37 East Seventh Street
New York, New York 10003
Visit our website at www.papress.com

First Princeton Architectural Press edition
published in 2016.

Special thanks to: Nicola Bednarek Brower, Janet Behning,
Erin Cain, Tom Cho, Benjamin English, Jenny Florence,
Jan Cigliano Hartman, Lia Hunt, Mia Johnson,
Valerie Kamen, Simone Kaplan-Senchak, Stephanie Leke,
Diane Levinson, Jennifer Lippert, Sara McKay,
Jaime Nelson, Rob Shaeffer, Sara Stemen,
Paul Wagner, Joseph Weston, and Janet Wong
of Princeton Architectural Press
—Kevin C. Lippert, publisher

Library of Congress Cataloging-in-Publication Data
La Farge, Phyllis.
The pancake king / Phyllis La Farge and Seymour Chwast.
     pages   cm
Originally published by Delacorte in 1971.
Summary: Relates the saga of Henry who, because he
could not stop making pancakes, became wealthy and
famous.
ISBN 978-1-61689-432-0 (hardback)
[1. Pancakes, waffles, etc.—Fiction. 2. Fame—Fiction.] I.
Chwast, Seymour, illustrator. II. Title.
PZ7.L139Pan 2016
[E]—dc23
                              2015027558

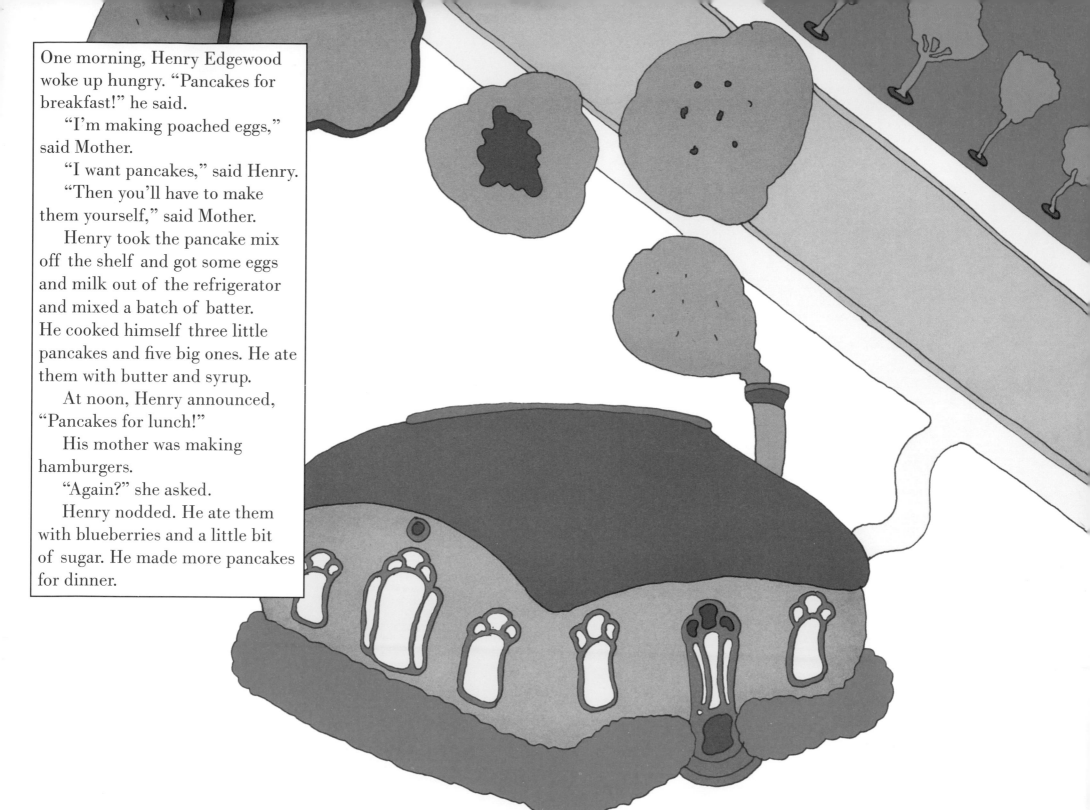

One morning, Henry Edgewood woke up hungry. "Pancakes for breakfast!" he said.

"I'm making poached eggs," said Mother.

"I want pancakes," said Henry.

"Then you'll have to make them yourself," said Mother.

Henry took the pancake mix off the shelf and got some eggs and milk out of the refrigerator and mixed a batch of batter. He cooked himself three little pancakes and five big ones. He ate them with butter and syrup.

At noon, Henry announced, "Pancakes for lunch!"

His mother was making hamburgers.

"Again?" she asked.

Henry nodded. He ate them with blueberries and a little bit of sugar. He made more pancakes for dinner.

From then on, Henry cooked pancakes three times a day: buckwheat pancakes, blueberry pancakes, cornmeal pancakes, onion pancakes, and even blini. He ate them with maple syrup, blueberry syrup, sour cream, whipped cream, and apple butter.

Henry loved cooking pancakes. The best part, of course, was flipping them. He got so good at it he could flip them with a spin right into his dog Ezra's mouth. Ezra was fond of pancakes. He was always right by Henry's side while he cooked them.

When Henry's friends Jack and Morton stopped by to see if he wanted to play baseball, he told them he couldn't.

"Why not?" Jack asked.

"I'm making pancakes," Henry said.

"In the middle of the day?" Then Henry's friends shrugged their shoulders and went off with their bat and mitts and ball.

But before long, Jack and Morton began to
stop by for pancakes in the middle of the day.
Old-fashioned flapjacks were their favorite.

The other neighborhood kids started dropping in
for pancakes, too. Even the mailman and the milkman
asked for some. Soon, Henry was cooking all day.

He invented new pancakes—strawberry pancakes,
coconut pancakes, bacon pancakes. He flipped them
higher and higher. Sometimes he gave Ezra's such a
flip that the dog had to leap into the air to catch it.

Often there were ten or twelve people in the
kitchen. Henry's mother had given up trying to do
anything except wash the dirty dishes and keep the
syrup pitchers full. Henry's father had to wait for a
seat at the table when he came home from work.

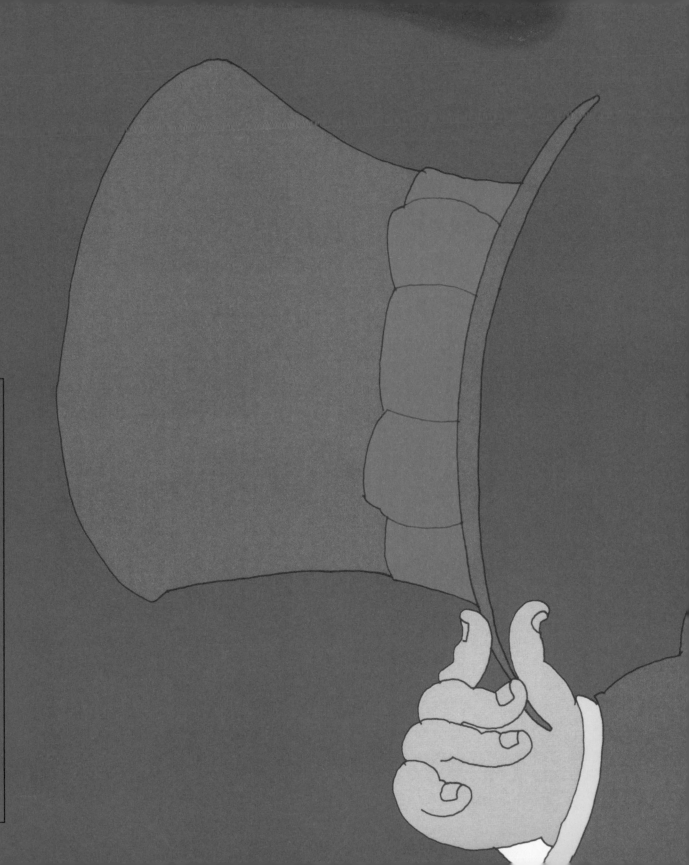

One day when Henry was making a batch
of Swedish pancakes, the doorbell rang.
A man in a blue suit stood on the porch.

"My name is Jinker," he said. "Arthur
J. Jinker of Jinker Enterprises. Is this
the home of the pancake boy?"

"My son, Henry, does make pancakes,"
said Mother. "Would you like to try one?"

"Don't mind if I do," said Mr. Jinker.

"Henry," Mr. Jinker said after his first
bite, "your pancakes are sensational."

Henry was not sure he liked Mr.
Jinker, but he said, "Thank you." Ezra
definitely didn't like him. He growled a
low growl until Henry told him to stop.

While Henry began to mix some new
batter, Mr. Jinker said, "This pancake thing
could be very big. If we partnered with
the syrup people, anything's possible!"

"We?" Mother interrupted.

"Henry and Jinker Enterprises, of course," Mr. Jinker replied. "Henry will be the Pancake King!"

"It all sounds very exciting, Mr. Jinker," Mother said, "but I need to talk about it with Henry's father."

"I understand, Mrs. Edgewood," said Mr. Jinker. "Here's a contract. Nothing too binding. Take a look, and I'll be back tomorrow."

That evening, Mother and Father and Henry talked.

"I think it could be a real opportunity for Henry," said Father.

"I'm a little afraid," said Mother. "Henry is so young."

"I'll still make pancakes for you and Father," Henry said.

The next morning Henry signed the contract, and everyone shook hands.

Mr. Jinker outfitted Henry in green trousers, a white shirt and apron, and a chef's toque. He gave Ezra a gold collar with his name stamped on it. Ezra tried to shake the collar off, but he couldn't. A photographer took pictures of Henry mixing batter, flipping pancakes, and smiling with a spatula in his hand. He even took pictures of Ezra catching a pancake in his mouth.

Henry was on his way! He and Ezra rode on their own float in the Marvel City Hometown Parade. Henry cooked pancakes as fast as he could, flipping them into the crowd. He even flipped one that landed right on the mayor's bowler hat. After the parade, Henry made crêpes Suzette for everyone. The mayor gave Henry a certificate that said "Marvel City's Very Own Henry Edgewood, the Pancake King." Three drum majorettes gave Henry a bouquet of red roses. Henry didn't know what to do with them, so he gave them to Ezra. Ezra ate them.

"I'm proud of you, Henry," said Mother when he came home.

"I didn't know you could cook them so fast or flip them so fur," said Father.

"It was easy, " said Henry.

The next day, Henry's picture was on the front page of the Marvel City Gazette, and the day after that he was mentioned in the Chicago newspapers.

A few days later, the president of the Easy Daisy Pancake Mix Corporation asked if Henry would be interested in making pancakes at the Easy Daisy Pancake Cook-In. He flew Henry, Ezra, and Mr. Jinker out in a private jet and drove them to the event in his limousine.

Henry made hundreds of pancakes. At the end of the cook-in, he was exhausted.

From then on, a day didn't pass when Henry wasn't doing a television commercial or at the very least cooking pancakes for a ladies' club luncheon. There were Henry Edgewood Pancake King fan clubs and Henry Edgewood Pancake King posters and buttons and Henry Edgewood Pancake King dolls. Sometimes when Henry made an appearance, the crowds were so big that Ezra had to go ahead, growling and barking to make a path for him. Disc jockeys across the country played "The Pancake King," a song written especially for Henry. "I'm going to flip, flip, flip for Henry!"

Now that Henry was rich and famous, he didn't see his parents much.

One day as he was crisscrossing the country, visiting the forty-three restaurants of the Pancake King chain, the White House called to ask whether Henry could get there in time for brunch. There were some international ambassadors coming, and the president wanted to serve them something really American. He said he would send Air Force One.

Henry got there just in time to make an extra large batch of batter.

But soon after Henry cooked pancakes at the White House, things began to change. He missed Mother and Father and Jack and Morton. He hadn't seen them for weeks. He missed playing baseball. He even missed school.

Not only that, Henry was beginning to have trouble with his pancakes. Some days they came out heavy. Other days they were runny.

One day when Henry was a guest star on a TV show, someone in the audience threw a pancake back at Henry after he flipped it to him. "It's soggy!" the man shouted.

After the show, Mr. Jinker said, "Henry, what's the matter? We can't have this. Your pancakes are our bread and butter; they have to be perfect every time."

"I want to go home," said Henry.

"What's wrong?" asked Mother when he walked in.

"I don't want to make pancakes anymore."

"But you have to," said Father. "You're in business."

Mr. Jinker pleaded with him. "You're rich and famous," he said. "We're counting on you. You can't stop now."

"Yes I can," said Henry, and he went up to his room and closed the door.

The only person who didn't plead with him was Ezra. Ezra sat at the foot of his bed and wagged his tail.

Mr. Jinker decided to leave. He'd heard about some three-year-old triplets in Saskatoon, Canada, who could sing lullabies while they did a juggling act.

After Mr. Jinker left, Henry stayed in his room for a few days longer. Mother put a glass of milk and a plate of cookies outside his door every now and then. That was all Henry wanted.

Jack and Morton came by every day to see how he was.

Then one morning, Henry woke up hungry.

"Come on, Ezra," he said.

In the kitchen, Mother and Father were eating boiled eggs.

"I'm having waffles for breakfast!" Henry said.

Henry's Famous Pancake Recipe

½ cup butter
1 oup whole milk
1 cup flour
2 teaspoons baking powder
¾ teaspoon salt
2 tablespoons sugar
2 eggs

Heat a griddle or cast-iron frying pan over medium-high heat.

On a separate burner, melt the butter with the milk in a small saucepan over low heat. Once evenly melted, set aside to cool a little, so the eggs don't cook when you add them.

Whisk the flour, baking powder, salt, and sugar in a large bowl.

Beat the eggs so they are evenly mixed in a medium bowl.

Now add the butter and milk mixture to the eggs and stir until smooth.

Add the egg mixture to the dry ingredients and combine only until the dry ingredients are well-moistened. Don't mix it too much; lumpy is good!

To invent new pancakes, you can add berries or sliced bananas.

When the griddle or pan is hot, add a little butter. For each pancake, fill a ¼ cup measuring cup and pour most of the batter onto the griddle. Cook pancakes until bubbles form and pop, and the bottoms turn golden brown. Flip with a spatula and cook the other sides until golden brown.

Serve to the mailman and milkman with butter and warm maple syrup, or flip one right into your dog's mouth!